This book belongs to:

Gaenslen

Jim Henson's
Muppet Babies
Count
with Me

by Louise Gikow   illustrated by David Prebenna

One Muppet Baby
hopping up and down.

Two Muppet Babies
climbing all around.

2

3

Three Muppet Babies
painting and sewing.

Four Muppet Babies
swimming and rowing.

4

5 Five Muppet Babies
slipping down a slide.

Six Muppet Babies
going for a ride.

6

Seven Muppet Babies
dancing and singing.

8 Eight Muppet Babies laughing and swinging.

9

Nine Muppet Babies
making mud pies.

10

Ten Muppet Babies
all in disguise.

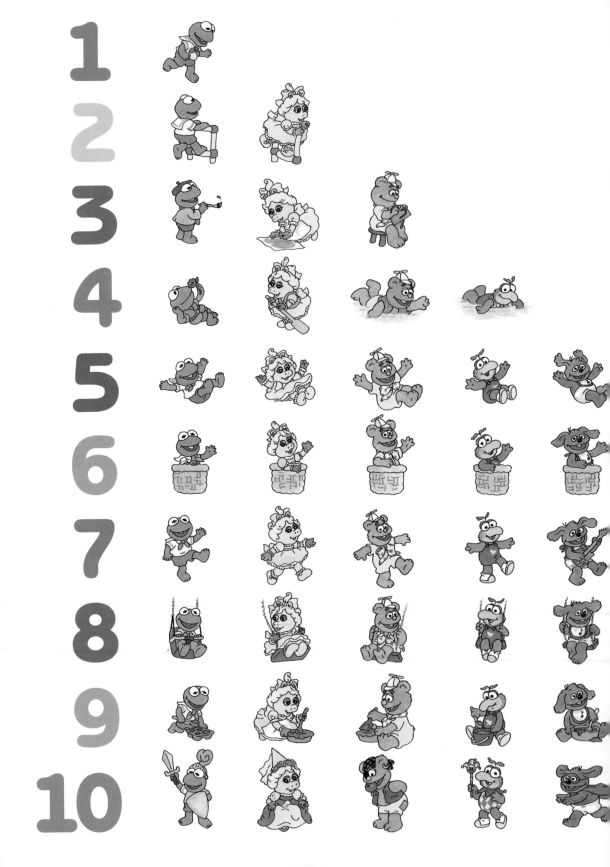

You've counted Muppet Babies
from one to ten.
Now, take a deep breath...
and do it again!